Miss Rumphius

Story and Pictures by Barbara Cooney

A TRUMPET CLUB SPECIAL EDITION

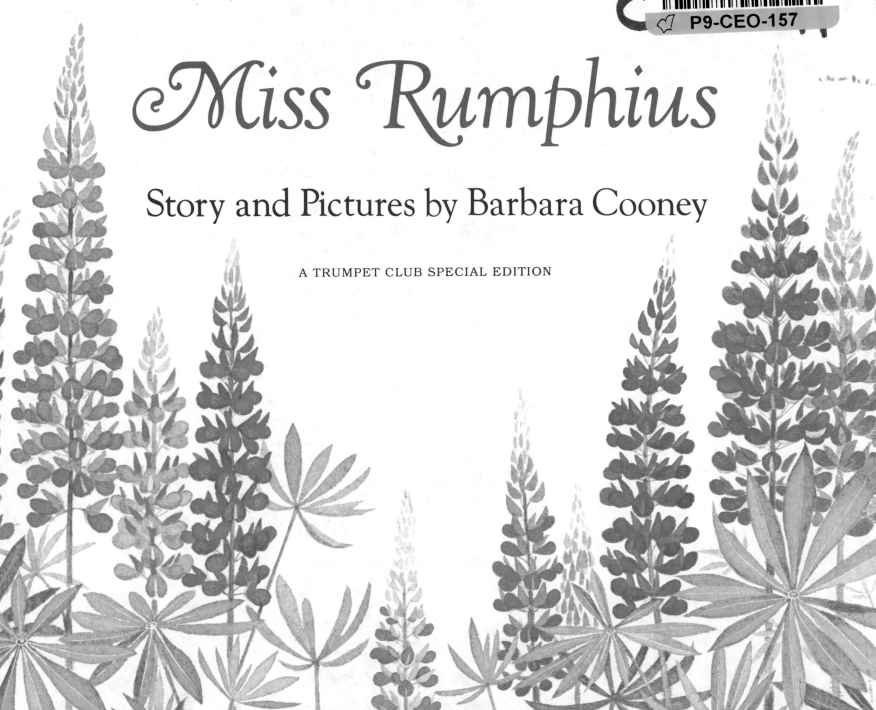

Winner of the American Book Award

Alice Rumphius wanted to travel the world when she grew up, and then to live by the sea—just as her grandfather had done. But there is one more thing, he tells her: she must do something to make the world more beautiful. Young Alice does not yet know what that will be...

"A strong feeling for Alice's independent spirit shines throughout the book yet is tempered...by the peace and beauty of the landscapes." —*Horn Book*

"From the Victorian rooms of childhood to the serene coastal views of old age this adventurous life is captured...with love and delicate brush strokes...dedicated to the belief that life and art are inseparable." —*The New York Times Book Review*

Published by
The Trumpet Club
666 Fifth Avenue
New York, New York 10103

Reprinted by arrangement with Viking Penguin Inc.
Printed in the United States of America
September 1988

10 9 8 7 6 5 4 3 2

To Saint Nicholas, patron saint of children,
sailors, and maidens

The Lupine Lady lives in a small house overlooking the sea. In between the rocks around her house grow blue and purple and rose-colored flowers. The Lupine Lady is little and old. But she has not always been that way. I know. She is my great-aunt, and she told me so.

Once upon a time she was a little girl named Alice, who lived in a city by the sea. From the front stoop she could see the wharves and the bristling masts of tall ships. Many years ago her grandfather had come to America on a large sailing ship.

Now he worked in the shop at the bottom of the house, making figureheads for the prows of ships, and carving Indians out of wood to put in front of cigar stores. For Alice's grandfather was an artist. He painted pictures, too, of sailing ships and places across the sea. When he was very busy, Alice helped him put in the skies.

In the evening Alice sat on her grandfather's knee and listened to his stories of faraway places. When he had finished, Alice would say, "When I grow up, I too will go to faraway places, and when I grow old, I too will live beside the sea."

"That is all very well, little Alice," said her grandfather, "but there is a third thing you must do."

"What is that?" asked Alice.

"You must do something to make the world more beautiful," said her grandfather.

"All right," said Alice. But she did not know what that could be.

In the meantime Alice got up and washed her face and ate porridge for breakfast. She went to school and came home and did her homework.

And pretty soon she was grown up.

Then my Great-aunt Alice set out to do the three things she had told her grandfather she was going to do. She left home and went to live in another city far from the sea and the salt air. There she worked in a library, dusting books and keeping them from getting mixed up, and helping people find the ones they wanted. Some of the books told her about faraway places.

People called her Miss Rumphius now.

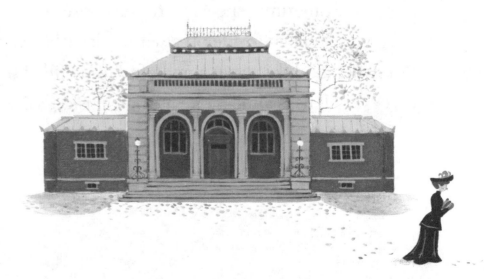

Sometimes she went to the conservatory in the middle of the park. When she stepped inside on a wintry day, the warm moist air wrapped itself around her, and the sweet smell of jasmine filled her nose.

"This is almost like a tropical isle," said Miss Rumphius. "But not quite."

So Miss Rumphius went to a real tropical island, where people kept cockatoos and monkeys as pets. She walked on long beaches, picking up beautiful shells. One day she met the Bapa Raja, king of a fishing village.

"You must be tired," he said. "Come into my house and rest."

So Miss Rumphius went in and met the Bapa Raja's wife. The Bapa Raja himself fetched a green coconut and cut a slice off the top so that Miss Rumphius could drink the coconut water inside. Before she left, the Bapa Raja gave her a beautiful mother-of-pearl shell on which he had painted a bird of paradise and the words, "You will always remain in my heart."

"You will always remain in mine too," said Miss Rumphius.

My great-aunt Miss Alice Rumphius climbed tall mountains where the snow never melted. She went through jungles and across deserts. She saw lions playing and kangaroos jumping. And everywhere she made friends she would never forget. Finally she came to the Land of the Lotus-Eaters, and there, getting off a camel, she hurt her back.

"What a foolish thing to do," said Miss Rumphius. "Well, I have certainly seen faraway places. Maybe it is time to find my place by the sea."

And it was, and she did.

From the porch of her new house Miss
Rumphius watched the sun come up; she watched
it cross the heavens and sparkle on the water; and
she saw it set in glory in the evening. She started
a little garden among the rocks that surrounded
her house, and she planted a few flower seeds in
the stony ground. Miss Rumphius was *almost*
perfectly happy.

"But there is still one more thing I have to do,"
she said. "I have to do something to make the
world more beautiful."

But what? "The world already is pretty nice,"
she thought, looking out over the ocean.

The next spring Miss Rumphius was not very well. Her back was bothering her again, and she had to stay in bed most of the time.

The flowers she had planted the summer before had come up and bloomed in spite of the stony ground. She could see them from her bedroom window, blue and purple and rose-colored.

"Lupines," said Miss Rumphius with satisfaction. "I have always loved lupines the best. I wish I could plant more seeds this summer so that I could have still more flowers next year."

But she was not able to.

After a hard winter spring came. Miss Rumphius was feeling much better. Now she could take walks again. One afternoon she started to go up and over the hill, where she had not been in a long time.

"I don't believe my eyes!" she cried when she got to the top. For there on the other side of the hill was a large patch of blue and purple and rose-colored lupines!

"It was the wind," she said as she knelt in delight. "It was the wind that brought the seeds from my garden here! And the birds must have helped!"

Then Miss Rumphius had a wonderful idea!

She hurried home and got out her seed catalogues. She sent off to the very best seed house for five bushels of lupine seed.

All that summer Miss Rumphius, her pockets full of seeds, wandered over fields and headlands, sowing lupines. She scattered seeds along the highways and down the country lanes. She flung handfuls of them around the schoolhouse and back of the church. She tossed them into hollows and along stone walls.

Her back didn't hurt her any more at all.

Now some people called her That Crazy Old Lady.

The next spring there were lupines everywhere. Fields and hillsides were covered with blue and purple and rose-colored flowers. They bloomed along the highways and down the lanes. Bright patches lay around the schoolhouse

and back of the church. Down in the hollows and along the stone walls grew the beautiful flowers.

Miss Rumphius had done the third, the most difficult thing of all!

My Great-aunt Alice, Miss Rumphius, is very old now. Her hair is very white. Every year there are more and more lupines. Now they call her the Lupine Lady. Sometimes my friends stand with me outside her gate, curious to see the old, old lady who planted the fields of lupines. When she invites us in, they come slowly. They think she is the oldest woman in the world. Often she tells us stories of faraway places.

"When I grow up," I tell her, "I too will go to faraway places and come home to live by the sea."

"That is all very well, little Alice," says my aunt, "but there is a third thing you must do."

"What is that?" I ask.

"You must do something to make the world more beautiful."

"All right," I say.

But I do not know yet
what that can be.

ABOUT THE BOOK

The illustrations for *Miss Rumphius* were painted in
acrylics with accents of Prismacolor pencils on gesso-coated
percale fabric mounted on illustration board. The art
was camera separated and printed in four colors. The
text type is Goudy Old Style, and the display type is
Goudy Cursive.

With thanks
to Hilda